The Fall of Heartless Horse

by Martha Kinney

LITTLE HOUSE
ON THE BOWERY

Akashic Books
New York

Published by Akashic Books
©2004 Martha Kinney

Grateful acknowledgment to Sutton Publishing and Oliver Thomson for permission to print quotes from *The Great Feud,* and to Mark Strand for permission to print quotes from *The Story of Our Lives.*

"Heartless Horse at the Glee Club," "Ambuscule's Factory Calculations," "Tadiscule Follows Ambuscule Around the Factory," and "Heartless Horse and the Offspring Problem" originally appeared at www.canwehaveourballback.com; and "Young Capitalists" and "Heartless Horse's Memo of Defeat" originally appeared at DMQreview.com.

ISBN: 1-888451-73-4
Library of Congress Control Number: 2004106240
All rights reserved
First printing
Printed in Canada

Little House on the Bowery
c/o Akashic Books
PO Box 1456
New York, NY 10009
Akashic7@aol.com
www.akashicbooks.com

for my father, with love

TABLE OF CONTENTS

Dramatis Personae

Heartless Horse: The Patriarch

Mrs. Heartless Horse: The Matriarch

Tadiscule: The First Son

Ambuscule and Minuscule: Siblings Rarefied

The Trembly Bird Who Flew Away: The Lost Daughter

Grandvikings: The Grandchildren

The Landscaper: Lover of Mrs. Heartless Horse

The Hatcheck Girl: The Mother of Heartless Horse's Other Child

The Soprano at the Glee Club: Heartless Horse's Lover

Donald Dhu: Delicious Bad Boy Long Gone

The Fall of Heartless Horse

Heartless Horse was on a fool's errand in search of a modicum of peace in the living room.

A premonition: an ambush of balled socks. Were this to occur, a terrible headache.

Mrs. Heartless Horse was game for quibbling but Heartless Horse was not. The facts are by no means clear but certain truths persist:

It was necessary to have a bigger navy than anyone else.

It was necessary to own huge tracts of land and a ring of powerful stone-built castles.

It was necessary to procure the Stone of Destiny.

It was necessary to procure a genuine leather-top all–cherry wood desk.

Heartless Horse looked over his traveler's clock out his window at the Bayou. Long gone were the high rocks of Dunnottar. Life was a fool's errand, landing him in Florida, far from the ambush of stones and daggers and closer to the ambush of balled socks. O Stone of Destiny. Little grains of sand. Little loud and shitting grandvikings riling him up! Hail Lame Heartless Horse! Swarmed by his pesky descendents. Gone were the days of the Galley of the Stern Rudder. The tailgate falls off. Follow the birds.

The Family Goose
There is a dire shortage of docile sheep!

From his office chair in the sky, Heartless Horse is resisting a family mutiny. He prepares his next memo: **The goose that has laid the family eggs for 100 years will not be sold!!!!** Down below, brothers and sisters are jockeying for position. They have developed a catapult for hurling dirty laundry onto enemy lawns. In-laws have been seen wearing illegitimate undergarments at various ice-cream parlors. The arguments for selling the family business are Minuscule, Tadiscule, and Ambuscule. The moon is wearing a dunce cap. It's the end of the wild frontier.

A Trio of Fiendish Voices Kept Heartless Horse from Sleeping at Night

Voice One: Tadiscule:

I, Heartless Horse, for one, am for the Tadiscule. If you are going to perambulate around, I believe, at best, it can only be fictitious to wear laundry, and imply a suppository of ham beyond belief. This just cannot be done at the expense of the family. It is unacceptable, intolerable, and uninhabitable. Think of the nephews in their vests having to defoliate points A, B, C, F through H, and point Q. It's plain immoral. Tadiscule immediately and be done with it!

Voice Two: Minuscule:

I agree, Heartless Horse, but would add that the Minuscule is essential as well. A complete distribution of the Minuscule is the only compassionate, legitimate, and percolate thing to do at this tincture and juncture to prevent a puncture in what seems most imminent. To add clauses 136D through 256FF might delineate the necessary underwritten bifurcated separation of aero, euro, hydro, and necro economics. Pay the nieces as well!

Voice Three: Ambuscule:

Ambuscule!!! Ambush the old bastard, you fricasseess!!! Let's down the goose and crack the eggs!!! Go for the gold, I say. Enough of this bullshit. I, for one, prefer my wife to wear her own lingerie and to sleep at home. I say we kick the old horse in the ass. To the glue factory he goes!!!

in aria repetissimo arondissimo again and againissimo through the nightissimo . . .

Premonition of the Trembly Bird

Somewhere in this complicated city of white chalk marks
I discern a little white cabin on top of a mountain.
From its chimney, a single ring of smoke.
I am going there.

Heartless Horse at the Executive Power Lunch

Fornicating and crumpled in his hand was the letter from his daughter. She was off to marry that asshole Lame Small Pot! Heartless Horse had been rallying his scepter in the stars. Stirring the cups of high-class soup, so to speak. Counting his clubs, spades, and diamonds, ordering his kings, queens, jacks, and aces. Now Heartless Horse was releasing his car keys to the hatcheck girl and lying on the lobby sofa for a minute of sleep. His shoes were too small. His wife was still shopping. Heartless Horse was having trouble feeling the left side of his face. Was his ear there? His eye? Life was but a fool's errand. Gone was the Stone of Destiny. A ring of castles on the finest hill was but a shitty little grain. Armies encircled him bringing him aspirin and water. Would he be egged on to battle? He'd rather die! Call him a headless horseman! A mentally unstable king!

Heartless Horse Egged on to Battle

Would he be? . . . Never!
Call him a headless horseman! A mentally unstable king!
(Was his ear there? His eye?)
Heartless Horse was circling the corral.
Littering the lair of the beast.
If Ambuscule and Tadiscule can't teleate,
I won't capitulate. It's a long heritage.
I spent years, years of my youth in the dungeon
with no windows, doors, chairs, or toilets,
working and sweating and learning those machines,
fructifying those eggs, and now you want me to sell the family goose.
It just won't be done. Not for grandvikings. Not for nephews.
Think of Charles the Foolish,
after his long and glorious career,
forced to leap out of a burning castle wearing chain mail,
no loch below to cool him off.
After my long and glorious career
I will not be ambushed by a city of balled socks.
I will meticulously and assiduously recount the plan
from point A to point F, appealing to reason,
then rewrite the bylaws to extricate all in-laws.
I will calmly and coercively extricate the exit rows
and extradite the fashion show.
I will ply with boar slayings, viands, tinctures,
and Sister Euphemia's well-seasoned purse.
I will maintain.
Just how . . . is a mystery.
Leave it up to me.

To Be a Trembly Bird,

you have to go.

Even when you have no place to go.

Even when there is no one out there waiting for you.

Even when no one has sent you a letter saying come along.

You have to go.

You just cannot stay.

You have to leave your one little bed behind for good.

Even when you have no shape.

Even when you have no eyes.

Even when your skinny arms melt as you reach for the door.

Even when you have no voice to whisper,

"I really loved you and will always remember you."

What is out there,

way out in the lonely

and beyond?

Being Tadiscule, Esquire,

oldest and legalest of offsprings,
acquainted with legalese
(as well as the heretofore forthcoming potential inevitable
demise),
I submit humbly to place this measure,
for your perusal, at your leisure,
honorary siblings,
on the next supernumerary agenda,
but before the perusal of the purchasing of the largest navy acqui-
sition,
an agenda item put forth by one Heartless Horse,
our grand but outdated bestiary executive issue.

Please submit your signatures to my plan.

For each of the sons and daughter,
gaining relative amounts of ham
can fortify their castle.
Tadiscule, Esquire believes the fortress will be stronger.
And our heritage extended generations longer.

To Heartless Horse we write:

*Dole out the appropriate distribution to alleviate the pious poverty
that is upon your hardworking offspring, Heartless Horse!!!*

Tadiscule on Tack
On suppositories of Ham, a memo.

MEMO: A suppository of Ham beyond belief

TO: Ambuscule and Minuscule, Siblings Rarefied

FROM: Tadiscule, Esquire

RE: The pitfalls of salutation to Horse
                without affirmative action for Ham

- In this memo, I, Tadiscule, Esquire, rally us, Rarefied Siblings, past the expository absence of the Ham.

- We must move on Heartless Horse with said affidavit.

- To file an affidavit regarding this Suppository, three signatures from all parties, although not mandatory, regulatory, or hereditary, would be perforatory to this paper.

- Please Note!! The procurement and extrication of said Ham from Horse is not to be confused with the ongoing hereditary deposits into our nocturnals, which shall remain forthcoming, in spite of heavyweight existential protubering on the part of said Horse.

- I shall prosecute if such a case should occur.

- While we shall remain salutary and divine in our epistolaries with said Horse at all times, respiting, reprieving, and pardoning of said Horse is prohibited.

- Before the taking of tea, please sign and remit to the heretofore Power of Beacon assigned.

From the office of Tadiscule, Counsel, Legalese
RE: The POSTPONEMENT of THE SIGNING and
REMITTING of THE HAM

Enter a New Concept: Tabling the Chairman

In dethroning the Heartless Horse, the Executive Authority shall be vested in the three vassals to exterminate a resolution of ham into an emergency; which may be delayed because of the passage of a motion to postpone to a time certain.

It is essential, vassals, I submit as your leader, and esquire, and epistolary fraternal, for this part of our longevity, to prepare an agenda for the legislative session, for example, in detail, to chair a motion to table the Chairman until further conversion of resolution could percolate a heartier plan contained in the original motion while suspensions of the rules, under Council Rule 1003 requires a vote of 2/3 of ancestors present and voting, according to rules of clothing, the motion to postpone to a time, debatable, could throw the plan and remit the desired ham, while tabling a chairman, in partial motion, could produce an amended table of contents in no means edible.

One cannot table an amendment, unless the measure which it is attempting to amend is tabled well, and well-furbished and garnished. A motion to table without hams in a situation of given heretofore desperation would be out of order. A motion to reconsider requires a majority vote while suspension of ham has been tabled and said chairman will automatically withdraw the ham and the measure to a safe kitchen where it can be weighed and stored.

This can be accomplished in three ways:

- A motion to lay on the table by said chairman.

- A motion to chair on a day when certain flocks are flying and eggs are to be had.

- A motion to withdraw to certain bedrooms and reconsider ham.

Agenda Addenda From the Law Offices of Tadiscule, Esquire

Please ruminate!!!!:::::
<u>Heartless Horse will not obfuscate if we do not procrastinate!!!</u>

We gain, siblings platonic,
by nuzzling the Horse,
a hefty momentum in our argument:

Furthermore, an adjudicating tactictiary tactic:

Far be it wisely for me to propose:
The Ham may be divided judiciously into three lots:

UPPER HAM
LOWER HAM
NOVA HAM

Each lot supervised by one sibling.
Each sibling acting as governor and tax collector.
Not eating the Ham but collecting the tax of the Ham.
Thereby preserving the Ham as the honorary Heartless Horse so desires but providing each of us with income.
Each of us not the OWNER PROPER of the Ham
but the GOVERNOR of the Ham,
the SERVICE REPRESENTATIVE of the Ham,
THE SPEAKER OF THE LEGISLATIVE COUNCIL for that portion of the Ham.

We get to nibble the Ham.
That being said,
no **GNAWING** of the Ham.

Please sign and remit.
I, Tadiscule,
the natural hereditary distributor and contributor,
must embark upon this legalese,
do hereby thank you for your tender,

T.E.

Let Me Go
Postcard from the Trembly Bird

I do not want the ham I want to be heard

I want the woods.

I want the birds.

Echoes down the path.

Echoes down the path behind me under the fallen leaves,

footfalls.

Echoes of footfalls under the fallen leaves fallen and falling forever

down the path behind me as I flee.

Flee back to the first land where we drifted;

the clouds unpacked their secrets;

bloodshed, brothers dead,

greed, insatiable need,

we were an autistic country in perpetual summer;

blooming over the Atlantic as we came.

Waiting for the King's Trumpet to Call Them Home

Two little vikings perched in the trees, high above the woody copse, whispering each to each. Made out by moonlight in the branches' v's. Little vikings plotted lifetimes of demise. I will marry a pirate and disappear at sea. I will lose a leg in an ambush and get gangrene. Who can bloody up the worst and gain honor? Who can marry the worst soggy dog of a man? How about a slow quiet death by happiness? Marry a clerk from Brisbane and eat peaches? How about a one-tooth one-eye gin-cracked knuckle-nosed grave-digger who had a knack for pissing in his shoe? A headless horseman charged through the castle gates on summer nights. On July 12th, approximately 11 PM, two vikings learned to fuck in a beech tree. Wildebeests made romper room in the grasses and the ice-cream truck came and went. No money was spent. Egged on to battle by Wild Scots, Charles the Foolish, wearing chain mail, and his lover Harriet the Small were forced to leap out of the burning castle to cool off in the loch below. There the ancient bell of St. Fine still rings its lament. In the best tradition of wicked aunts, Sister Euphemia the Weary locked the girl in a room without food and water.

Heartless Horse at the Glee Club

The glee club meeting

                                    true rollicking

the bollix of it all;

                              he was not stalled,

he felt a heigh-ho, and a fourteen again —o;

        he was a fine kind of base   with a handsome face

ta ta ta tum heartless horse in the musical jam,

                                    there was a slam,

              a cantankerous fun kind of plan,

altos ate jello,

singing accapello,

in the stairwell,

oh the mystery was fairwell,

farewell to trouble,

this lovely musical bubble,

oh did you know,

how lovely oh,

oh the sound of tenors ah la la ing,

he was set free ing again and again ing,

he was to be ing,

feeling his oats, his jelly, feeling quite free

feeling the glee of it all when he first heard the trill

a lovely soprano thrill in a red velvet dress

sang the Scottish briggoon and he swooned

and float ing the room ing and soon he was gone ing

was go ing was flow ing

ta ta ta tum the beat of a drum

she was fun   she was a plum   she was the one . . .

Ambuscule's Factory Calculations
Siblings, listen up!

I'm a mechanic and a Busimatician,
good at business and logic, a magician.
These machines here are a little outdated.
They aren't balanced and weighted
with proper yolks and lines.
Horse doesn't know that I have devised
New Eggs for the New Millennium.
Please watch. Ambuscule, the Mechanic
and Business Matician, can help you
provide a proposal that will soothe the Horse
and provide ample eggage for the causal roles.
Thirteen fragments put into solar figments.
Give a third of a ration backed into a portion
would give us each one more vacation.
It's part of an ambush plan.
These machines, to oil and slick,
put the wrench into the bolt hole and then add
the subtractions with the fractions for the proper calculations.
Put the wrench into the bolt hole, turn to the left
with a quarter screw. Three hairs above the oil line
gives the egg a cracking split.
Each for one of us, plus two.
Turn the clock to a minus the mid-hour and set.
Take these firing arms and blast the Horse's rutts.
This will down the old machines and get him
where he needs the Busimatician's getting.

If you like my plan then mount the bus.

Tadiscule Follows Ambuscule Around the Factory

Mm, hmmm. Good point, Ambuscule, good point.
But will council executive take it well?
Will heretofore search and seizure of this row of applications
meet the Horse's requirements for a new moniker bell?
Yes, yes, the eggs weigh well with your new measures
but to extract our most efficient pleasures . . .
(Ambuscule is not refined in the matters of the mind
and I must bode my time to lay these plans to deeper platters.
Longevities should be applied.
The ground should be widened
for the machines have gotten shorter and fatter.)
Ambuscule, Tadiscule does intuit large reformations at hand
in order to remit us tonnage vis-à-vis products libelous ham.
Could we not line your weight with this yolkage to the date
of the disquisition a little longer and wider?

Brilliant move, Ambuscule!   Then, to the bus!

(I see I'll have to do this on my own;

                                        —when it comes to brains,

there's really only one of us!)

Heartless Horse and the Offspring Problem: A Focus Group

Heartless Horse is in the boardroom, conducting his last stand,
flanked by a retinue of expensive bankers, lawyers,
and now the addition of an annoying family therapist:

"I assure you, sir, combine . . .   *simple psychology* . . .

                    therapeutic sessions . . . prevent

these needless regressions

            . . . business *training and strategy* . . .

                                    you too can *recover*

                    calm and loving *community and order* . . ."

Let the consultants bleat on.
History is bloody repeating itself, there is no stopping it.
Scots. Always had numbers of unruly sons,
pillaged and murdered each other,
                                    a preternatural condition,
. . . all desperate for a piece of the pie . . .
                                    why, in 1687 . . .

The ungodly fact persists; his boys . . . they are small,
small in the head, small-minded, small-winded, smally imagined,
they are weak, wobbly, defective, and they cannot be sent back,

back to where?! back to the sheep farm?
back to the factory, the Lady Rock?
Only one of them smart
and *she* is a mess.
Flew off like a trembly island bird and never came back!

No, the boys are soggy. Thick in the head. Poorly read.
And their pronoun problem!
A conversational hazard!
An embarrassing mess!
Me and John are going to the bank.
Me and John!!
Not *me and John,* you bloody fool!!
John and I!!
How indeed had he come by these?
No, education isn't what it used to be
but neither are the genes, Heartless Horse,
since the clerics first whipped vitae from the boll.
The commission of fire and sword is no more.
The problem with offspring: they just don't spring off.

The Bloody Claymore Bearing Brothers

That's we! The Bloody Claymore Bearers. Brothers to the end, we're fearsome and free. We changed the style of Highland fighting and brought the English to their knees. We sailed the seventeen seas. Stormed the pirate hideaways. Stole the Commission of Sword and Fire. Now our father is leading us onto the mainland. We are taking the castles by force. We dismember the lands. Divide and conquer. Gain mysterious claims to fame. Gather potatoes. Cop milk from cash cows. Build the Hoover Dam. Straddle the Grand Canyon. Amend the Constitution. Steal Lady Liberty's pussy. Our new headstrong young king, flexing his muscles, laden with booty and prisoners, the slight taint of regicide still lingering, expensive retinues of hereditary poets, doctors, and lawyers in tow, partakes in our monastic movement's distilling of aqua vitae, the strong spirit, *fire water*. And through a small window in the front door of our fine new mansion in our gated community where we revel and fuck madly *whomever* we please, including small girls by the name of Harriett the Small, Beatrice the Lost, and Geraldine the Ugly, food is passed to exiled and starving uncles, occasionally, on a rainy night.

Too Good for Me
Song of the Trembly Bird

O Donald Dhu,

                             I have a crush on you.

               Half-Macdonald, half-Campbell,

You win my spurs,

                                You fight like a cur,

                                       drink liquor.

With a long sheet of black hair, you boycott the fair.

                                 I wait for you there.

Where did you come from, baby dear?—Out of everywhere, into here.

How good was Good John?—Too good for me. Too good for me.

O Donald Dhu,

                                        the bells ring over the water.

The castle gate is locked.

                              The branches are cold and bare.

The ice on the ground is the only sound.

                                              O Donald Dhu,

I have a crush on you.

My schoolyard is no more.

                                         You keep score.

                        I see your galley on the night air.

                                                    Row me there.

The Lonely Strains of Mrs. Heartless Horse went Trailing through the Trellis and once again were lost over the Moat on the Nightly Breeze . . .

Dreamed she stormy pillars

                                    dreamed she salty weather

thrashing water

                      cherry leather

to come   to come

he promised to come home early from work and fuck her

                                              but

again he never called her,

                      never came

working late again.

                  He was a thief.

                                              She

                  needed to

be stroked.

Ahh Stormy leathers ahh

                  filthy fun pillars

call her a wench, a black bitch, convict her of witchcraft!

                 Be she yoked   be she stroked

                         dreamed she of the

black-haired pirate mmmm   from the islands of

Rum

and

Egg;

             Yum   Yum

                     what else could she do?

             Strum

She had been lying lonely in bed for decades.

Strum

Heartless Horse should have died on his wedding night.

Strum

A pompous equine.

Strum Strum

Men and their castles and land.

Strum strum strum

A woman has her cravings.

She dreamed of the pirate from the islands of Rum and Egg

with a patch on his eye,

his salty smile, ahhhh mmmmmmm

and his nimble hands.

Lah lah lah ahhhh

He captured ships,

marooned groups of impotent fools on small rocks,

pleasured the women,

and

strum,

cast their useless husbands off to sea.

O divine god. O. O.

O, Holy shepherd.

Tender of the needy.

My mad and horny pirate,

O, Stormy weather, thy staff

and thy rod they comfort me.

Lay me down

        lay me down beside the thrashing waters

while my greedy property-obsessed husband

        wails lashed to his ring of stone-built castles

ahhhhhhh

          ahhh large fleets orgasms thrash me

thrash me O secretly thrash me loud

        and salty thy rod thy comfort

          against stormy pillars my pirate sink me

sink me in a posse of stormclouds

O, muscle me in your thunder and lightning,

O, bury your treasure in this motherland, O landscaper

leave the lawn alone

                                        yes, stop mowing

            get in here and fuck me, yes

                              yes, stormy pillars

yes, salty weathers

                                    thrashing waters

            and yes, on the equine's all-cherry leathers,

                        yes, yes, the sea

                        and the smell of gasoline

yes, carry me

                        tarry me . . .

Young Capitalists

In a far recess of summer
Monks are playing soccer.

The sun's brown bodies tumble down and into the water the swelter of turquoise cool wet wealthy thrashing. Down, down, under to gather the coins, to plunder under to gather the coins, to plunder the treasure, to scrape up the glinting silver, to brush away the worthless copper. Smartest and biggest and longest, we hold our breath the farthest, finning the fastest, we clean out the deep end down down where the big coins lie, surface them and pile them in our one sneaker left poolside a soggy purse in the splash. Our loot. Our cash. Winner takes all. We take tans, sun, heat, hot cement, lemonade, calm days, high dives, skinned knees, smoothed thighs, feeling better. Better than him, better than her, better than your mother's yellow sweater. We win swim meets, races, hopscotch, money-dives, b-ball, t-ball, softball, badminton, ping-pong, four square. We see fireworks, town parades, art fairs, circuses; we lie in the grass, play in the zoo, and ride the horse in market square. We see a movie, write a play, build a bicycle, bake a cake. Winner takes all. We take heat, hot cement, lemonade, calm days, high dives, skinned knees, and golden thighs, feeling better. Better than him, better than her. Better than our mother's newest sweater. She is a go-getter.

The Epistolary Interviews

Newby Tuttle Talks Teleology with Tadiscule, Esquire

From the Desk of Newby Tuttle, PhD.

To Tadiscule, Esquire

The World Renowned Philologist and Celebrity Interviewer Newby Tuttle

Humbly Requests to Correspond with Tadiscule, Esquire,

In an Interview to be Published in *The Family Hackensack,*

the Prominent Magazine of National Repudiations.

Please Respond Accordingly.

Sincerely,

Newby Tuttle, PhD.

From the Law Offices of Tadiscule, Esquire

Memo to Newby Tuttle

Please submit your suppositories of ponderance

to the heretofore Power of Beacon assigned.

Hence and yours, truly acquitted,

T.E.E.F.

The Interview

Newby Tuttle:
I offer, humbly, the following questions to Tadiscule:
Nietzsche? Pro or Con?

Tadiscule:
My dear friend Newby, Nietzsche was,
as is our dear patriarch, Heartless Horse,
whom we love and adorn with emulations,
and whom you perhaps deviously
have come to find us
tearing at the mane of
through our interfamily repudiations,
but you will not find us destroying,
perhaps only reemploying in new pursuits
more zealous to his age's hosieries,
Nietzsche was amiss, wandering from God,
needed more daily sleep, underlying dental work,
but he was otherwise a SuperFossil.
To quote him: *"I teach you the Super Ham."*
Pro! A supernumenary momentum!
"Morality is the herd instinct in the individual."
Pro again!
We feel no guilt in the procurement of what is rightfully ours!
Tadiscule, Esquire, Epistolary Fraternal,
having been employed in the procurement of the Family Ham,
begs to differ, however, with the legendary blend on one point:

Counsel differs on said quote:
"Ham is something to be surpassed."
Con! Nietzsche, listen in.

When certain flocks are flying and eggs are to be had,
nothing *mounts and straddles a good breakfast better*,
provided there is a preponderance of normal ham. *"God is dead,"*
but we have procured a ring of stone-built castles
and are proceeding along certain legal and tender perforations
to the tabling of our Chairman in a partial motion
where said Chairman will be weighed and defoliated by the Court,
in a sudden reverse appeal transmitted to the Right Honorables,
affidavits filed, master-moralities and slave-moralities reversed.
Yet nevertheless and not heretofore neglected we heed your wis-
dom, Nietzsche,
for *he who fights with Heartless Horse might take care*
lest he thereby become a Heartless Horse.
Tuttle, we are not filly-fallying around here,
as dapple offspring often do.
We have heard stories of HH and the hatcheck girl,
and take care to go to church to prevent our generation's
further following in such a posse of the patriarch's derelictions.
In-laws have been proceeding with prosecutions and tales
in divorce courts, tape-recorded whinnyings, naysayings,
and late-night rompings about pastures felonious,
Heartless Horse's hoof prints on foreign bedspreads,
erroneous confederations of jealousies
and omelets appearing in false genes,
Tadiscule does enumerate the preponderance
of Nietzsche heretofore foreknowing of these.
Strange gallopings across the sovereign bestiary.
We shall prevent our family's repudiation
by giving him an excavation
and then a lengthy vacation.
Thus ends my answer to your inquisition.

Newby Tuttle:
Some days I have no idea if a belief in God is valid or simply a crutch.
I wander around feeling like a jerk. Any suggestions?

Tadiscule:
"*Is God out there?*" Blind man, we're not bowling alone!
Tadiscule will not loiter with your pandering.
He convicts you, tularemic brother, of tumefying,
of wandering the tumulous playgrounds and sowing your sour sausage
every which way in the wind.
However, while you are out there with swine and the Gadarene Demoniacs,
dangling a carrot in front of an empty seesaw might prove something.

Tadiscule does recommend some Total Quality Management and staying in crosswalks.
If you be growing hooves, it might behoove you to get on your knees.
To quote my friend Jesus, "*And why are you anxious about clothing?*"
In search of his excellence, the great G.O.D.,
seek freedom in Someone Else's Authority,
seek Power of Beacon from one heretofore-appointed Prior in his white salty nightie.
With minimal fees to T.E.E.F., I may direct you to our pastor's inscriptions.

From our community experience, these Pastors Platonic do find:
calling on a personal nightly vision to be hallucinatory and digestive.
Let us pray. My wayward fish, I shall gather you in.
For example, before bedtime, some vigilances:
Let us visualize God as a swirling blue-liquid acid
in a rarefied Wellington tumbler
garnished with the Chairman,
one feverish squirming Heartless Horse,

50

barely afloat on a paper umbrella,
desperately calling to us for our prayers,
swirling in the swill as he goes down.
It is only then, Christians,
that we can act in our lordly nature's true benediction,
being graciously salvatious,
and pluck our loving hands down
and save the equine from his bestial ineptitudiary inflations.
Supremely divine.
We go to church on Sundays in our felt orderlies
and herald our hosannas to that velvet day.
Hip hip hooray!

Sinners, gather round.
Tadiscule, Apostolary does sense a demurral.
Perhaps Newby Tuttle is in need of a referral.
He is demountable from his PhD. which affords him a tertiary J.O.B.
However, he himself admits he needs a healing of paralytic pro-
portion.
Tadiscule does ruminate upon the dumb demoniac before us now.
Only an evil and adulterous mustard seed seeks signs.
As Jesus says, *"He who hears and does not do is an odd deposit."*

Perhaps, Newby Tuttle, PhD.,
you have been chewing too much freedom with your toast.
At the law offices of Tadiscule, you may seek your sign
in our pleotropic prisoner's box replete with chains and whippings.
Taste your freedom there and you will know God.
God is like the liver.
You never notice him until something goes wrong.
Nature abhors a vacuum and God abhors vacuum cleaners;
he believes we should sweep.
Fear of God can evoke coffee. Hot coffee is unreasonable.
It moves the bowels without suppositories or supplications.
However, the pastor as an American sheriff

in the litigation of prayers that may secure you
in the intestines of God's fig tree at the very least, this is statutory.
Do not be frothy or sweaty; be heartened!
Tadiscule does administer his own prayers to rally true purity,
and will accept application of all wayward crutches.
The palpitative facts: you have been an ad hoc plebiscite
keeping the finger in the dike but now this customized paint enhancer
and apostolic P.I.P. (Performance Improvement Program)
can administer the pleopod. We recommend the headlong pursuit
of ham.
Fun is optional but the prophets of gloomy earnestness get
hammered freely on Fridays.

Tuttle:
Golf?

Tadiscule:
Ahh, the fairways of Tadiscule's youth did tender him. These were
the daring and precious days when even Heartless Horse was a
carrier equine of engendering codification. Such imprintings were
divine and natural, quite hereditary indeed. Days of youthful,
when one young Tadiscule did with Ambuscule gambol there in
sunlight elegiac and play lapidary through the fairway's blue legis-
lations. Across the emerald portfolios, ever profiting from the blue
airs and having little cares but the smacking of the featherie,
young fraternals sliced and diced at the lawn's maternal mounds
making magical brown mouths, and traveling, yes, Tuttle, south,
south along the sand traps toward the sun's sweet glimmerings.
However, dear Tuttle, be not mistaken: many of life's lessons were
procured and inured in these pleasurable flotations. It was there in
ticklish pleasures we became young men worthy of vacations. We
learned that one must drive the ball down the center of the fair-
ways of life. And it was there that Tadiscule learned the most fun-
damental Dentals of life: Play Quickly: Slow Play Is Rude. No
Putting out of Turn. Make Certitude You Ascertain Your Head Is

Down, You've a Strong Grip, and Your Left Arm Straight in the Administration of a Good Firm Stroke. One Must Always Address the Ball Properly. Sinking a Long Putt Is Mandatory. If the Ball Is a Long Way from the Cup, then Bearing a Pleasant Smile, Tiptoe Over, Shade Your Slander, and Pick it Up.

Tuttle:
Where do you get your ideas?

Tadiscule:
Ahh, Tuttle, vitriolic! You exacerbate a break and entry into *the illuminati*, the treasure chests of Tadiscule! Tadiscule, Esquire does visualize you now, clear as a bubonic dawn: your undergarments slip, your tongue flips, as Tadiscule did predict; be he heartrended to reckon this has always been your intent. Salaciously, you have lubricated the trough, and now you want to suck my sources up. Why do you ask? *For whom do you work?* I have not seen *The Family Hackensack!* Before this inquisition, I searched the confectionaries far and wide, but none had report of such a tutelage. *Has one Heartless Horse put you up to this?* I shall place detectives on heretofore search and seizure, with attached pending indictment, prosecution, conviction, and ending with unpleasantry breathalyzer applied at entry into penal saddlebag. I shall study your bank numerologies, trace your heredities, sunder your philology. If you are unverity, you shall be repudiated. If not, I am untremulous to iterate, my sources are inspirational and convocational, and derived on my daily constitutional. I channel the greats, from Sun Tzu to Billy Graham, who have spoken to me through daily visualizations, voicings, whispers, and smells of ham. But I'll say no more. Furbish your credentials, and perhaps on further subjects, we shall consider our potential.

Tuttle:

Why?

Tadiscule:

Tuttle, the question is not "Why?" but *why* "Why?" Philologist, let us unpack your suitcase. To eviscerate your ponderance, we will detonate your package. Are you weighed and measured too sincerely by your PhD.? Desire you to play footsy, Newby Tuttle? Your question brings me back; I do reminisce early days of jamboree when I did pedestrian my young Minuscule to school, and she, sisterly, would ask me, "Why? Why? Why?!" As I did dressage ahead toward learnings weighty, I do admit areas of befuddlement and percolation at such a hesitation of the young filly dallying in the walkway behind me. "Why? Why? Why?!" she would berate. I did agitate. Perhaps by "Why" she did imply: let's not continue to edifice with daily calendars and structures of instruction and tutelation; instead, let's pillowfight! Let's plunder feather together! Let's play in white snowy weather! Over there on the dells of blue hills. Let's over this lovely purple mountain range to eat stacks of cakes blueberry and syrup, be fried buttery plated! To be loosified together. In rarefied weather! And why and why and why, indeed! But such a young Lincoln was I, buckled into my studious epiphany, and headed for my filigree, as you heretofore know me, I could not stop and be pleasured. I continued in responsible measure. And poor young Minuscule was roped in to square roots; had she a fraction of my mental capacities, she should have played more and studied less. Be she only worthy of tincture preparations now, and the occasional darning of a dress. So, Tuttle, let this interview be an instruction for you. Your sudden question "Why?" betrays your nature, which may be more childish than based in reason's measure. Perhaps it would suit you not to publish this interview at all, for who in the end will be repudiated?

End of Interview

Heartless Horse Babysits

Monster–O–Lithic!

                              Little viking.

                                        Such a tongue!

On a boy.

                    Young tot's large licker leaves large hole

              there for lately a boy's long tongue can

                                        roll drum roll!

How big is Big Boy's Tongue?

                         Is it a paddle, a Large Leaving, a Hole?

Such a hole's leaving

Is Large,   A Pole,   hmmmmm . . .

Opens a role for Horse to play!:

In Awe of the Awful Tongue

(Squirm like a worm, Horse, in terror replete)

of the child's chin down so low

eyes the long protruding

begins his brooding,

Even the Horse's liquor is stunned

The Eyes roll back,

Above the tongue

Two huge eyes enlarged

Swirly monster pop inventions

Attempt to attend the convention,

Of horror

leading or glotting

follow the pink carpet

to the tiny chin

unrolls jelly whole

tongue fun

Masterful,

        its assertive hypoglusion,

                its profusion

This kid,

       He's plum with his tongue.

He's masterful!

        He's mine.

             (One of my line)

              He's Tongerkind.

Minuscule Up in Arms over the Naming of Grandvikings

If he names his little viking *Archibald* . . .

If Tadiscule so much as dares to name that little tuft of mouse fur
that he calls a boy's head *Archibald* . . .

It sounds too much like my sweet little viking boy *Harchibald!*

It just can't be done!

My *Harchibald* is the only one!

We shared sweaters, tans, summers, even weather,

we shared and shared

and now I'll share no more;

it's time for keeping score!

Think back: Tadis, Minus, Ambus . . . it was *AWFUL!!!*

My little Harchibald will never suffer;

he'll be the only ibald of the Horses or . . .

we'll be rivals;

we'll be metals;

I'm telling you it's bad now,

but I know frog spells;

With Beupleurium Cornucopias coming out of his feet he won't be
able to sleep

I'll withdraw my Rescue Tonics,

my Kava Kava, my Valerians,

my Toe Revitalizing Creams

I'll give him a Bubonic!

I'll withold tinctures, pleated quilts, plaids, and skirts

and better yet!

I'll produce him

a Pharmacopoeia Dystopia

that little fur head won't forget!

Heartless Horse at the Golf Tournament

"Fudge it, Freddy!!

                                    You're making an ass of me!!!

I shouldn't have used the nine iron!!

                        I told you Freddy, I should have used the five!

Of course it was going to land short!!

                        GOD DAMN IT WHAT DO I PAY YOU FOR?!!"

Another stupendous day on the green

                        Heartless Horse and berated caddy

            Shimmering sunlight, glittering flags, luscious trees.

"It's fine, Freddy, don't worry.

                        My fault.

                        Well planned on your part.

                                    Poorly executed by me."

A classic Scottish plot. Pretend to retreat

                              while moving to higher ground

from which he gained momentum to unleash a crushing charge:

"JESUS CHRIST!! WHERE THE HELL
DID YOU GET THE NOTION

                          A FIVE IRON WOULD WORK ON THAT?!!"

Just so

            the remarkable dysfunctional duo

                         of caddy Freddy and Heartless Horse

made their way across the rolling greens of the country club,

                   glorifying the golf tourney with his gandering.

Freddy, beast of burden,

wily,

tongue tied, tongue thrashed,

humped with clubs, silent, nodding.

Heartless Horse sweating,

numbed feet swathed at the grass in orthopedic sneakers,

rode like a king in cart behind.

Blue sky, fairways, far off, the sound of the ocean's tides.

The rules: clubs must walk: so, Freddy.

Horse, and only Horse, of all players in the tourney, could ride.

He couldn't feel his feet—

                              that silly neuropathy, and dammit,

it wasn't alcoholic no matter what they said.

All the other golfers walking hurriedly by,

                              he felt like a fool

and this damn caddy who had to scoop up all the titles in his leisure—

            a bloody genius who won every cup, just scooped it up,

helped the Horse now in no measure; a nine iron to be sure!

Mrs. Heartless Horse, as always, flitted past him too

in her tiny golf skirt, jewels, and bony old legs flirting

with her young partner

to scoop the lady's title up

while Horse, bald and grim, and undeniably last

sweating at the sun's coming setting,

innerly bemoaned the forthcoming downshowing

climbed the final hills of retreat

crossed the putting green

a complex man massive and limping

not what he'd planned to be

when he'd donated the money for the fountain.

On the Terrace Golden Leaf they were handing the young man, the winner,

and Mrs. Heartless Horse,

The Silver Bowls

She was   all smiles   charming   gracious to Behold.

Heartless Horse, besmattered in sweat, half in the bushes, shivered.

In the afterlude, while swinging his club,

a macabre twist

(not even swinging his club: handing it to his worn-out caddy!)

he sprained his wrist.

Executioner falls from horse and botches job.

A God thing?

Where was God?

There is no God. When you're dead, you're dead.

In retaliation, in the parking lot,

Heartless Horse fired Fred.

Making himself respectable once again

and escaping the inevitable

(as did many of his ancestors, a noble retreat),

in a leaky boat.

The Fated Gift

Grandmother Horse out shopping for trinkets

                  discovers a BLUNDERBUSS

perfect for her Pirate Lover,

                                    blackish

bulkish,

                         just rightish,

but should she buy it?

        Heaven's to Betsy!!

                The Horse's ducats are hers too!!

But oh!!!

                Such a lovely awning!

It looks like the sea—so aquamarine.

                              Reminds her of the isles of bells—

But this, here!!!

This thick black-belted leather

                              would buckle him up swarthy, salted.

Oh, hells bells!!!

                    I'll take it and stop my worry,

I am married to the Heartless,

                              After years of waiting and pratting

             I am worthy . . .

Heartless Horse's Memo of Defeat

Mrs. Heartless Horse was in love with a pirate landscaper.
His trio of fiendish offspring was off scheming.
His own policy of divide and rule had left him with no friends.
He had suffered the mutiny at the Lion's Club. He had no navy.
Rumors around town he had produced a bastard son with the
hatcheck girl.
(She was a furry dwarf!) (He hated the hatcheck girl!) (She chit-
ted, she chatted!)
(She was a heather twig-wearer always asking for token assurances
of safety!)
Murder of a brother-in-law might ease things . . .
(An act of revenge acceptable in Highland tradition . . .)
His bid for lost territories and titles had gone unheeded.
And he had yet to procure the all-cherry leather-top desk!

Heartless Horse wandered out to inspect his lands . . .
He hated his castle, built 100 years earlier on a site chosen by a
donkey,
where an ancient hawthorn tree still strangled the vaulted basement.
The private gaol where now he stored his defunct wine collection
was crumbling. A furry mouse scurried away.
A pseudo drawbridge over a dry moat.
A headless doll lay stripped in the sludge below.
Little grandvikings to and froe-ing on tricycles didn't even notice him.
He had a fancy for that one particularly cute one, didn't know her
name;
but she had cute blond pigtails and dimpled cheek . . .
she slashed him in the knee with her pink sequinned claymore;
(he buckled into the moat)
she rode on . . .

Memo: Famosus Libellus

To: Ambuscule and Minuscule, Siblings Fructified

From: Tadiscule, Esquire

Heartless Horse dost attempt to endow his Primary Hereditor, Tadiscule, Esquire, with one said libelous disclaimer which traveled to the Law Offices of Tadiscule, Esquire in a woolen sock via postal service carrier. The sock aggresses your Honorable Fraternal and refuses Ham.

Horse plans to outwit this Esquire in a battle of wits and sentiments. Be forewarned. He approaches your domiciles feigning a whiplash injury from falling into the moat where he claims he was whipped by one tiny grandviking feminine. Wearing a white hulkish hospital pad about his equine's décolletage, he attempts to gain our pity and to keep Ham.

Be it said: Give him Pity but not Ham.

Tadiscule, Esquire does refute this planned fee tail and will proceed with Ham procurement as planned. The image of the ferae naturae of our patrimonial in a tear-glazed testimonial does not dissuade me from the course I must take for future generations of Esquires and Epistolaries.

Fiat Justitia

Loss at the Stove Top Ford

It was a remarkable victory, much romanticized.

Cast your plaids
Draw your blades

The night partiers captured the rocktop castle. Tiny home Vikings, balconied, ambushed attacking Highlanders, hurled crumpled dark ale cups, makeshift claymores, and cigarette butts. Salty Nancy screamed for mercy from the 9 o'clock bridge, and further minor slaughter. A Don Juan turned an old trick of lady acquisition, became an overnight musician. There was dancing on the roof, leaving kilts and plaids flung over the moon. The sympathetic piper paid for his music with the loss of his hands. Plunderers in roving bands. Massive quantities of livestock were consumed. The infamous fracas and mutiny in the kitchen. Came one son of the King, carrying shield studded with brazen knots, all plaited and plumed, leading the fray, appeared mounting his dubious steed to stop the Horrible Deed, but the enemy was famously nineteen, and six-foot-three: he was no soft opponent, and son of the King could not. Lame Larson had his head in the spaghetti pot.

Grandmother Horse

Mrs. Heartless Horse brings the girl a trinket.

Above the crib she lingers, attempting to play

with the girl, so there it dangles

—the ugly trinket,

a mutation in pink and gold

—but the girl does not see it.

The tiny grandviking is pink with screeching.

Her fists are purple as pomegranates.

She is weeping but has no fever.

She is weeping but has no cold.

Has many toys. Has clothes and food and water.

The grandviking is wet but has

clean diapers.

Why is the grandviking weeping?

Outside the bells of St. Fine are ringing.

The sun is glistening over terra cotta rooftops.

The grandviking is small and getting smaller.

A tot without toddling, her legs are getting shorter;

she is not walking; she is not talking.

Voices of little vikings skipping to school.

Mrs. Heartless Horse dreads these visits.

What is wrong with Tadiscule's tiniest viking?

Where is Mrs. Tadiscule?

Tadiscule Putting at Dawn

Tadiscule's wife is not well.
No, Tadiscule's wife is not well and he plays in the lapidary,
he plays the blue ribbons of dawn, the gray fairways of dew,
makes everything even the gone of his forever-flighting wife
new, but Tadiscule at dawn again, alone: wondering what to do.
He must be harder on her; he must practice disquisitions;
he must buckle her down into his certainties soon.

Tadiscule mustn't tarry with these weightless ponderings;
he must work the blue legislations of early dawn,
smacking the featheries quite rightly
to bring him soundly and vigor.
Then be home to do the raising of the young fillies.
For his wife has off to plunder powder
and the weather is bells the weather is matted with the history
of these leavings this hell she has taken,
and given, his not well wife, trembly and shaken, her black eye,
and he thought he hid the bottles well,
he thought, under the wheelbarrow on the lawn . . .
She is a crimson Tremolo . . . she gets high on the placebo . . .
and the fillies, swollen and crying, cannot be rocked to sleep.
His concise prosecutions have rendered guilty verdicts nonetheless.
It's hopeless . . . He must maintain, however, for the sake of the
rest . . .

Heartless Horse's To Do List

Send two eagles to the Prince of Wales.
Tape up windows.
Parquet the street.
In God's Hands?
Nonsense! Someone has to do these things!
Leave a message for the wrong son on the wrong machine.
Shuffle across to kitchen for some aqua vitae in bare feet.
Good to be doing business from home.
Damn it, Mrs. Heartless Horse!! Batteries for my Traveler's Clock,
Please!!
Issue some commands: to caddie: Polish Clubs!!!
Landscaper: Less Fertilizer!!!
Good to have the lay of the land.
Yes, of course, every fiefdom needs its king.
Be Economical!
Leave message re:
No more financing son-in-law's folly.
This precludes calling for a new TV.
No more dabbling in debris:
Castle crumbling:
Kingdom succumbing to universe of malls.
A God thing?
Cancel Christmas Claymore order for naughty grandvikings!!!

The Legend of the Red Hand
And on fall days Horse gamboled with his fillies in the park

Football, in the park, with Horse

                The foot race

Run it as fast as you can

Racing your brother,
Cut off your own hand
Throw it far in front of you to win

                                        Possession

Possession of the piece of land

                      Possession of the wind

You have to win
You have to win the Horse's hand
You have to win the running across the grass
In touch football the flag is the rag and tear yourself

                                            Free
Free near the posts of the trees where you run and run
With the ball you must tag that tree, you must prove you are fastest

        Cut off your hand, do what you can you must win

You are The Red Hand flying on the wind.

The Bloody Hand born on the air.

Possession, touchdown, out of bounds,

Throw your hand,

Throw it red and bloody,

Siblings lost to you, groped and bossed,

Whatever the cost,

You first and muddy,

Little Red Hand,

Trembly bird, Lost:

Knuckle the wind.

The Proclamation of the Ham: Further Agenda Addenda to Restore the Faith and Soothe the Mane of HH

My Siblings Suprarara, My Offspring Proxies,
My Speakers of Provolone Plantations,
As legislative directors, Tadiscule, Ambuscule, and Minuscule, agree:

- To suppress self-inflicted scurrilous insurrections.
- To retail interior tonnage, vis-à-vis tort claims act entrailings.
- To define and punish interhousehold piracies and felonies committed on the high vacancies and offenses against the law of sitting.
- To emit bills, coinage, and the twig-wearer's torn corset.
- To develop one of the largest navies desired by Heartless Horse.
- To exercise exclusive legislation, the migration or importation sum toto in tort.
- To privilege habeas corpus of hired family therapists.
- To Edict.
- To Edify.
- To Decree.
- To the Editor in Chief, a legible Summary.
- To Educated geese shall fly just west of the ferry landing.
- To Educationalists frustrated with our planning.

In The Provinces of Ham
Heartless Horse shall be exalted *then* remodeled.
We shall assure him:
Even in moments of high caloration there will be:
- No capitation.

- No offspring shall lay any duty of tonnage; keep troops or ships of war.
- No Bickerings or Panderings at Legislative Confederations.
- No Tenderizations of Heartless Horse's Personal Locations.
- No Counterfeiting of the Ham.
- No Naturalizations of Neuropathic bottoms or ends.
- No Rotations.
- Few Flotations.

Instead, Laws, Laws, Laws,
Laws for Harmony, Euphony Well-Done,
and the Silent Implementation of the Tranquility of the Bun.
Laws for:

- Beacons
- Ferns
- Tender
- Quarantine
- Ferries
- Dredges
- Laws for Go cart races.
- Laws for pronouns in their places.

All assets connected with such portions of P. of H.
assumed by local leader to be tendered respectively.

Let us be Orderly and Governly.
Let us be Literary.

Sincerely proposed and legislated,

T.E.E.F.

Donald Dhu, No Soft Opponent

as if this were still the age of chivalry

She was his main target,

                              born to be

in spite of her father's words . . .

              If you stay out of the sewers long enough
                   you might stop meeting rats.

                        It was a summer day. The sun never set,

and Donald Dhu,

              with his flair for doing the unexpected

                              swapped it for a Ford truck.

Outwardly good-looking and polished,

Donald Dhu, the *Cochese,*

his favorite gun, his *Cuckoo,*

locked her up on his island of *Cannon,*

made girlie photos, nursed an obsession,

monster toads that lived in his dungeon.

The moon never glowed that night when little vikings,

fishing from their windows,

followed his singing over the sea.

In a Restoration period like Indian Summer

she was always his main target,

born to be.

On that fated night,

she swapped garb with the earl,

and was last heard of lodging cloud-born,

lithe and thrill as a bird,

remembering her father's words.

Minuscule's Ministrations of the Falling Horse

Fewer will be his fever if we ministrate with my mini
pharmacopieas; for my feverfews extol much efficacy in headaches
used to clear heat manifestations and a poultice to the cheeks of
Cnidiums: used for thousands of years by billions of people
for rebounding before lingering depletion sets in
to summon strong defense once cold or heat conditions . . .

Feverfew?

        It's not new!

                I'm telling you! . . .

I'm an herbal practitioner monography!

                    Listen to me!

Grandvikings!

Place these pillows of teas Chrysanthemum Parthenium
below his buttocks and elevate his ankle beams.

Marry a poultice of Gingko flavonoids and 6% terpene lactones.
Gingko lacuity tonic: combine gingko leaf with herbs traditionally
used to nourish Jing (deep reserves)
and works as a tonic for brain function,

increased cerebral blood flow and oxygenation.
Gingko Biloba—oldest surviving plant species on earth.
Increased circulation to the brain, arms, and legs . . .

Who am I?

I'm Minuscule!

The Herbal Midwife! *I went to school!!*

You!

Little Grandvikings!

Commence fanning application of this aromatic balm
to his nasal pharyngeal orifices with this eagle feather

Yes!
It's right!

For pallid complexion due to ham loss

and reduced appetite . . .

To The Doctoralis of Heartless Horse
As spoken by Tadiscule, Esquire, Epistolary Fraternal,
Upon the Downing of the Patriarch, Heartless Horse

Plenish your ear, please. Please be advisable that our Heartless Horse is widely perused for perambulings. One cannot play frick and frack with a power executive as if he is a leather sack. Furbish the proof he is stroked and not simply sleeping before attacking the capillary map with your generals and captains. We are a peaceful species and do not heretofore call upon your cannons unless they be necessary. Our mother is beside herself over this bestiary of chemical assaultings. Legislative measures are my meet and necessary foreboding if you do not heed our loathing on this perfunctory. As eldest fraternal, it is my meet to beckon your senior marshal. Granted the antechambers are dark, and outside is but stars, but rouse plenipotent marshal from his carbunckling, if you be certitude of your rendition. If you be certitude, I repeat, you best be rectitude! I cannot stress my inherent power brokerage's ignition! You will be charged with more than malpractice and sedition! You are an odd locket. No more of this tongue waving! Best follow instructions from one who knows of legislation. I repeat, rouse the leather general of instruction from his sack! The Horse is down! We must know of the real underpinnings before this ongoing attack. *But he's awake! The Horse is up!* Siblings prayered and met, gather round. Visualize how wrong you are, Doctor, and apologize, or be courtified.

Heartless Horse Lives on in Spite of Them All

"I tell you this, this robe of harmless flames I wear is no rich man's torn pajamas."

He'd had a stroke, so they said;
they wanted him dead!
He'd fled the hospital.
How far had Heartless Horse had to go
on his own, alone, how far?
Mother Horse had never been kind;
boney, beguiling, lost in her furs,
had never had time,
she had been no soft opponent,
obsessed with her illness
and with the red and green tartar,
she'd been a tsar.
How far had Heartless Horse had to go
on his own, alone,
he had sailed the seas
of commerce, factory, and conglomerate family
and for what, *for what?*
Heartless Horse, upon this thoughtful rambling
in the summer's heat suddenly looked up . . .
The shapes of all the clouds in the sky
did suddenly resemble him to the T!
They were stolid and bulky and dark,
then suddenly, and, quite completely,
broken apart!

Where do I come from? asked the trembly Horse.

*My father who fell into a vat of molten metal
is now part of a distant skyscraper:*

The galleys have sailed away.
The heat was stinging. The bells of St. Fine ringing.
He wandered out over the small bumpy hillocks down to the
bayou.
He was without friends, cast out on the lands,
without father, without mother, brother, without plans.
He'd had a stroke, so they said,
but he was alive!
"And when you find yourself where you will be at the end,"

(. . . *at the end* . . . that silly old poem . . .

                                    stuck in his head . . .

and he was alive! No time for silly poems!
Certainly he was no sun, no moon, no king, no planet, no star)

". . . tell yourself, in that final flowing of cold through your limbs . . ."

(God *help the Heartless Horse;*
his pulse? Damn it: fine!
It was hot but a chill ran through him)

                    ". . . *that you love what you are.*"

And So Will I
Postcard from the Trembly Bird

In the woods I hear birds; I hear animals weeping,

I hear people shrieking. I lose my way.

There are many nights.

Then there are flowers, summer showers.

There are boxes drifting in waves,

a boot, a mattress cast upon a hillside, scattered grain.

Someone is saved. I think I hear my father crying in the rain.

I do not go back.

There are castles in the water. There are castles in the trees.

I am floating to the new world I am floating on the breeze.

I miss you Horse. I miss your silence, your head rubs,

your nuzzles. You know things about me no one else could know.

I carry your mane inside me, weeping over the Atlantic as I go.

In my beginning is my end. Houses rise and fall.

Horses live and die.

Horses live and die and so will I.

From My Tree I Can See Them
Postcard from the Trembly Bird

scramble through submerged rooms,

over broken furniture,

trample tables with wild animal legs,

push through windows open to the moon,

and out into the horse's

blue apple orchard

where there are no apples,

but the great world

and the memory of his love

way out

in the lonely

and beyond.

The Trembly Bird Speaks
Where did we come from? Where did we go?

Once, long ago, I came sailing over the moat in a bucket,
and my hands were small and my feet were small
and my father ordained me: *little trembly bird that flew away.*

Little girl with little feet, little brown button eyes,
you are weak and cannot run across the street,
but I sailed across the grass in my bare feet,
many nights under the moon in my white night gown,
and I hid behind that tree, what fun it was to hear him calling me
home.

But lay up for yourselves treasures in heaven,

                    where neither moth nor rust doth corrupt,

and where thieves do not break through nor steal.

Our treasures: the wild of brothers now long gone,
a bb gun pelting my legs as I ran across the lawn, and this was summer, was heaven,
was the sweat of the heat and the suddenly moving faster and faster,
I leapt up on that butterfly swing on the elm, I closed my eyes . . .
higher and higher,

                    for where your treasure is,

there will your heart be also.

White moon, flip flops in the sky, slap, slap,
the sound of my breath moving faster, faster,
that hot summer night as I swung over the sidewalk and over the grass
of the parkway and over the clouds.
Consider the lilies of the field,

                                        how they grow:

        they toil not,

neither do they spin, but we spun, did we spin on that swing in the
summer night's heat night after night. *The light of the body is the eye:*

        if therefore if thine eye be single,

                                thy whole body shall be full of light.

The ocean, cool, clear, and deep.

                        Where did we come from? Where did we go?

We passed over shiny black stones and onto the sandy bottom,

                our feet skipping and hopping,

                                the light of our bodies shining forth.

Like water bugs on our backs, from the motherland we came;
we drifted across the skin of the dark water in search of a raft,
of land, of the new world,

our tiny floating tummies,

                        cast free,

                                    drifting for days,

the invisible lanterns of a vanished world.

Notes

Page 25. Waiting for the King's Trumpet to Call Them Home
Phrasings from *The Great Feud* by Oliver Thomson.

Page 34. The Bloody Claymore Bearing Brothers
The Claymore was the larger two-handed sword that came from Germany and changed the style of Highland fighting. Phrasings from *The Great Feud*.

Page 35. Too Good for Me
The Campbells and Macdonalds are two Scottish families who endured a lengthy and bloody feud. "Where did you come from . . ." —George Macdonald.

Page 44. Young Capitalists
Epigraph by John Ashbery.

Page 45. The Epistolary Interviews
"What can one person do?" —Bertrand Russell; "I had been chewing freedom with my toast . . . the prisoner's box . . ." —Albert Camus, *The Prisoner's Box*; "Fear of God can evoke courage." —Vaclav Havel, phrasings from Phillip K. Howard, *The Collapse of the Common Good*; "And why are you anxious about clothing?" —Matthew 6:28; Seeking signs: Matthew 12:38; Gadarene and Dumb demoniacs: The New Testament.

Page 61. Heartless Horse at the Golf Tournament
"A classic Scottish plot . . ." From *The Great Feud*.

Page 70. Heartless Horse's Memo of Defeat.
Phrasings from *The Great Feud*.

Page 71. Famosus Libellus

Famosus Libellus: a scandalous letter. A fee tail establishes a line of inheritance different from the normal one. Ferae naturae: wild beasts of nature. Fiat Justitia: "Let Justice Be Done."

Page 72. Loss at the Stove Top Ford

Phrasings from *The Great Feud*. Epigraphs from the same.

Page 78. The Legend of the Red Hand

A Scottish tradition and legend: One sibling racing against his brother has to reach and touch the stone first to win possession of a piece of land, cuts off his own hand, and throws it far in front of him to win.

Page 82. Donald Dhu, No Soft Opponent

". . . she swapped garb with the earl . . ." and other phrasings from *The Great Feud*.

Page 88. Heartless Horse Lives on in Spite of Them All

Epigraph from Mark Strand's "The Monument," page 94 in *The Story of Our Lives* (Knopf). Strand writes, "I tell you this robe of harmless flames I wear is no poor man's torn pajamas"; "The shapes of all the clouds in the sky did suddenly resemble him . . ." page 74 in *The Story of Our Lives*; "Where do I come from . . ." page 75; "My father who fell into a vat of molten metal . . ." paraphrased from page 75; ". . . when you find yourself where you will be at the end . . . tell yourself, in that final flowing of cold through your limbs . . . that you love what you are . . ." from "Lines For Winter," page 115 in *The Story of Our Lives*.

My general thanks to Oliver Thomson and to T.S. Eliot.

Other selections in Dennis Cooper's Little House on the Bowery *series*

GRAG BAG by Derek McCormack

203 pages, a trade paperback original, $14.95, ISBN: 1-888451-59-9

"*Grab Bag* culls the best of the perverse and innocent world of Derek McCormack. The mystery of objects, the lyricism of neglected lives, the menace and nostalgia of the past—these are all ingredients in this weird and beautiful parallel universe."

—Edmund White

HEADLESS stories by Benjamin Weissman

157 pages, a trade paperback original, $12.95, ISBN: 1-888451-49-1

"*Headless* is at play in the world. It is fearless, fun, and sometimes filthy. Weissman invites you into an alphabet soup of delight in language. Eat up."

—Alice Sebold, author of *The Lovely Bones*

VICTIMS by Travis Jeppesen

189 pages, a trade paperback original, $13.95, ISBN: 1-888451-42-4

"This book marks the debut of an author who will surely become a major voice in alternative literary fiction . . . rich, lyrical language reminiscent of a modern-day Faulkner informed by the postmodern narrative strategies of Dennis Cooper."

—*Library Journal* (starred review)

LITTLE HOUSE ON THE BOWERY